My Moving Day

Illustrated by Sarah Jennings

Picture Corgi

Read more books in this series:

The Friendship Bench

Show and Tell

Dinosaur Disaster!

MY MOVING DAY
A PICTURE CORGI BOOK 978 0 552 57608 6
Published in Great Britain by Picture Corgi,
an imprint of Random House Children's Publishers UK
A Random House Group Company
This edition published 2014

3 5 7 9 10 8 6 4 2

Picture Corgi Books are published by Random House Children's Publishers UK,
61–63 Uxbridge Road, London W5 5SA
www.randomhousechildrens.co.uk
www.randomhouse.co.uk
Addresses for companies within The Random House Group Limited can be found at:
www.randomhouse.co.uk/offices.htm
THE RANDOM HOUSE GROUP limited Reg. No. 954009
A CIP catalogue record for this book is available from the British Library.
Printed in China

Hello, I'm Molly.
This is my mum and dad and my big, bad brother, Oscar.
Oscar is usually muddy and greedy.
And this is my very special cat, Whiskers.
I have a lovely house with my own lovely bedroom.

Now, the thing is, Mum and Dad say we are getting a new house, which I think is strange. Why do we need two houses?

Then Dad says that we won't be living in this house any more.
We are going to a new house and we are never coming back!
I am very cross and Mum and Dad are very quiet.

Mum tells me about all the new things to look forward to.
The house will be bigger, my bedroom will be bigger
and there will be a little room for the new baby.
"Will Whiskers come with us?" I ask.
"Yes, Whiskers will like the new house – there will be a
bigger garden," says Mum. "Perhaps Whiskers will even
find some new friends!"

Maybe the new house will actually be amazing. The garden
might be so big that we could get a small pony for it –
or at least a goat . . .

These are some of the things I am packing
for the new house:

My rag doll

Pongo Pig
(he is not a
real pig)

My jewellery box

Molly

Some snacks
for the journey

On the big moving day my
friend Jessica comes to help
say goodbye to our house.

I am very sad that Jessica will not
be moving house too, but Mum says
that we will still do lots of fun things
with Jessica when she comes to visit.

When we get to the new house, it is NOT as big as I thought. If we do get a pony, it will have to be a very small pony. Maybe the size of a cat.

There are lots of boxes everywhere.
Will things *always* have to be in boxes
in the new house?

Whiskers doesn't like all the boxes – I don't think he
understands about the new house. I try to explain, but he
just hides. We have to keep all the doors and windows
shut to make sure he doesn't go outside and get lost.

I see a boy next door and he sticks his
tongue out at me!
How very rude. He might not be a friend.

Oscar helps me put some things in my new bedroom.
(Even horrible big brothers can be nice sometimes.)
But it doesn't really feel like MY room – it's just a room.
Pongo Pig does not like the new house and I think he
might be right. And where are my snacks?

Then I hear knocking at the door . . .

I go downstairs and see that boy
from next door looking in through
our front door.

"Hello hello hello!"
he shouts. "I'm Max!"
I run downstairs and say,
"Hello hello hello! I'm Molly.
Why are you shouting?"

And then I shout: "SHUT THE DOOR!!!"
But it is too late. Whiskers goes WHOOSH
out of the new front door and away into the
new street.

"Nooooooooooooooo!"

"Oops!" says Max.

I want to run to my room and cry. But then I realise my room isn't my room any more and I have nowhere to go. What if Whiskers is lost for ever, or hurt or borrowed by pirates?

"YOU LOST MY CAT!" I shout.
"I'm sorry!" says Max.
He does look sorry. But I'm still cross.

Mum and Oscar go and search under cars to see if
Whiskers is hiding. Max and I stay in the house.
Even though it was an accident, I keep on being cross
with Max. He has ruined everything!
Then Max says, "Come on, let's go and find Whiskers."
"We will never find him," I say.

"Yes we will," says Max. "I know – let's become cat detectives!"
"There's no such thing."
"There is!" says Max. "I'll show you."

So together we find the
dressing-up box.
At first I'm not sure, but
then we really *do* become
cat detectives. Although
I am more of a
cat-detective fairy.

We draw a map
of the new garden
to try and work out
where Whiskers
might be.

Then we look under pots, up trees and behind bushes.

Whiskers is not there.
He's not anywhere.

"I know, let's bring Whiskers back with his favourite things!" says Max. "What are they? Does he like robots? Dinosaurs? Remote-controlled cars?"
"No, of course not – he's a cat!"

"What does he like then?"
So I say all the things he likes:
fish, cat food, toy mice, cuddles . . .
"We can't bring him back
with cuddles," says Max.
"I know!" I say.

So we find some fish fingers, some cat biscuits and a toy mouse. We put them out on the lawn and then we hide. And we wait. And wait . . .

But Whiskers is still nowhere to be seen.

"Molly, where else could he be?" asks Max.
"What does he love doing most?"
"Well, his favourite place is my bedroom,
but that's a million billion miles away."
"But your NEW bedroom is here!" says Max.
"I think we should check."
I don't think there is any point in looking, but . . .

There, on my new bed, right next to Pongo Pig, is . . . Whiskers!
I jump on to my bed, curl up with Whiskers and give him the
biggest hug of all time. Suddenly my new room feels much
more like it is MY room.

To celebrate having Whiskers back, and our new house, we have a little party. Max and his mum and dad and big sister all come. I think Max is my friend after all. Perhaps the new house will be OK. And even if there isn't room for a pony or a goat . . .

I think there might be room for a small dolphin in the bath!